AF442398

The Lonely Bat

By: Krysteena Vycious

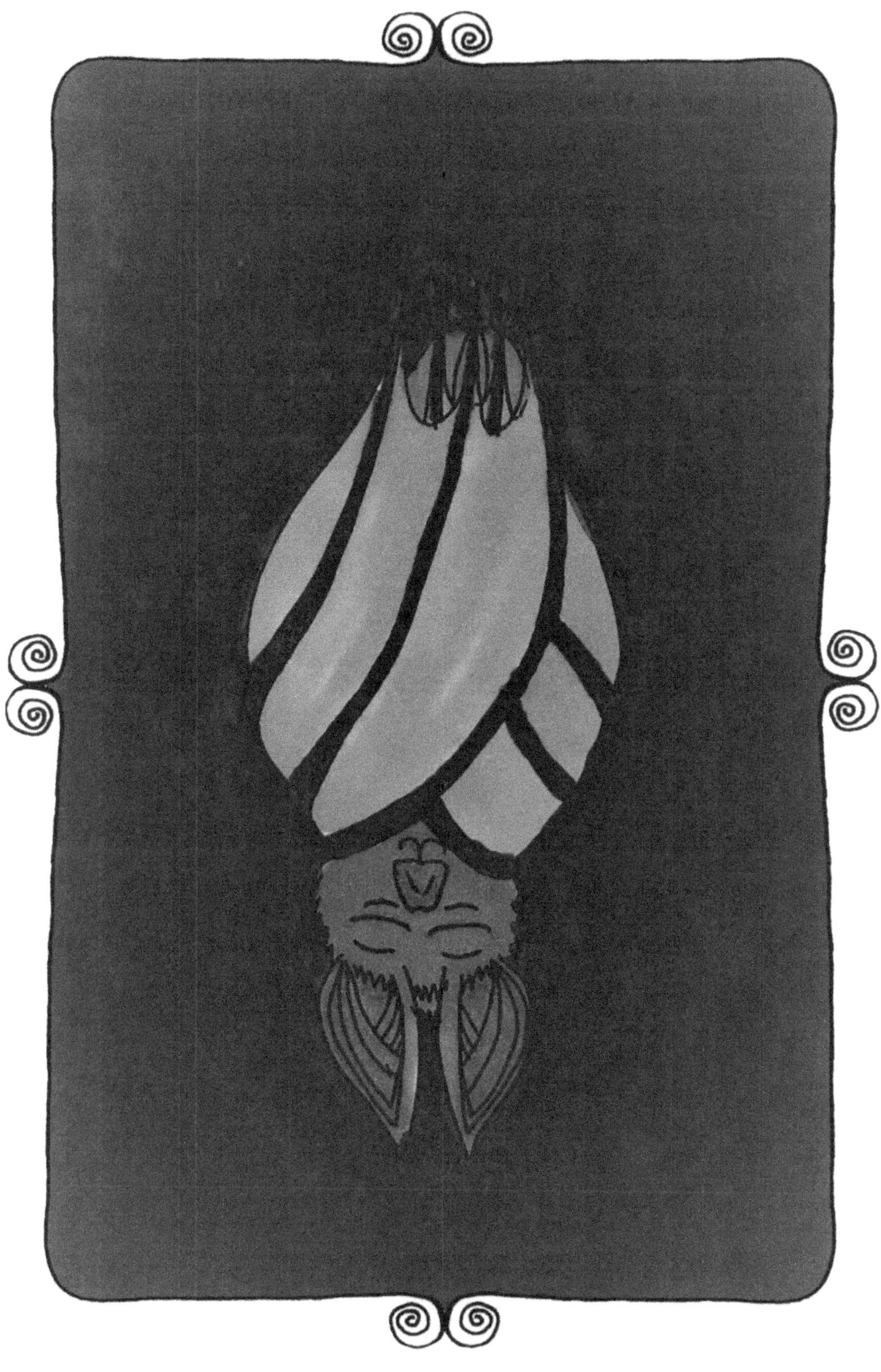

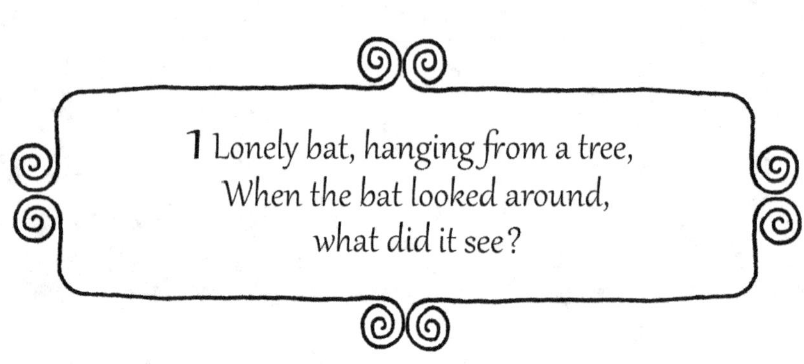

1 Lonely bat, hanging from a tree,
When the bat looked around,
what did it see?

2 spooky ghosts, dancing on their graves

II
RIP
2

3 Jack-o-lanterns light their way

4 Scarecrows Watching,

IV

4

5 Owls on the hunt for mice,

V

5

6 Hungry cats think,
dinner would be nice!

7 Scared mice, scurry up the road,
into the house...

VII

7

VIII

8

9 Gargoyles look on from up high

IX

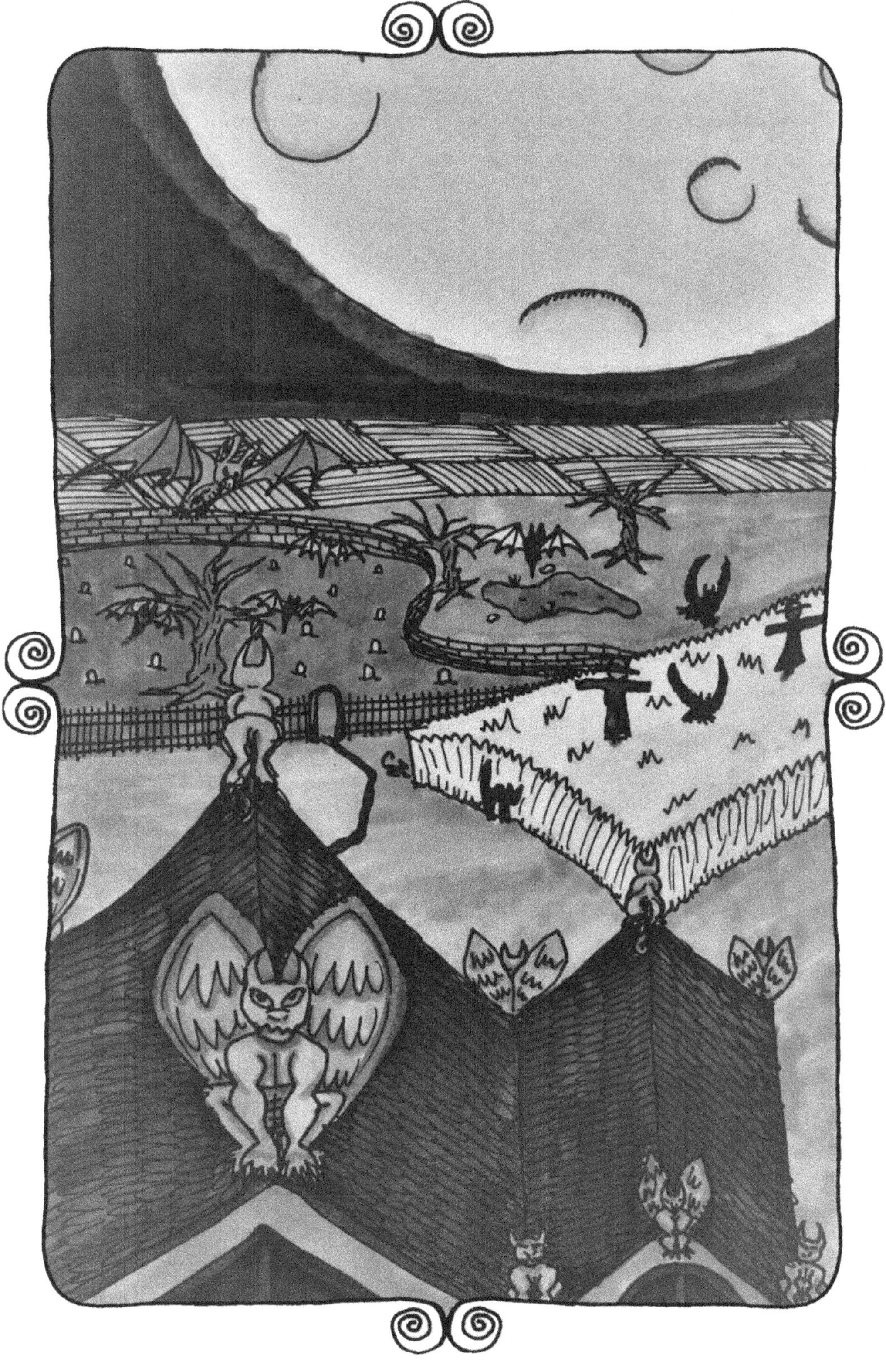

9

10 More bats go flying by...

X

10

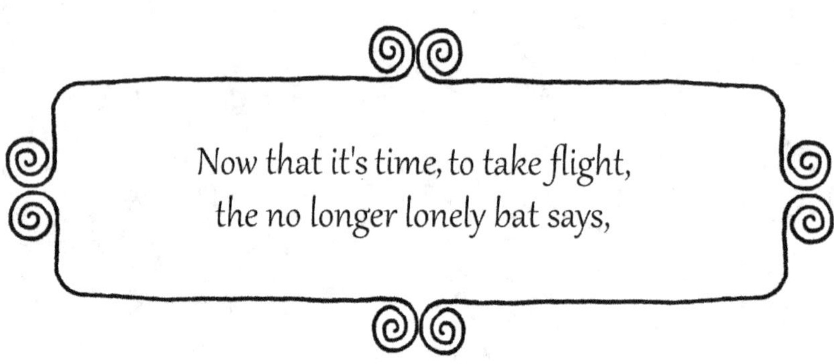

Now that it's time, to take flight,
the no longer lonely bat says,

Goodbye and Goodnight!

THE END

Vycious Arts Studios
Baltimore, MD 21213

www.ingramcontent.com/pod-product-compliance
Lightning Source LLC
Chambersburg PA
CBHW080730120726
48001CB00010B/3188